GYMNASTICS
is for me

Rosemary G. Washington

photographs by
Alan Oddie

 Lerner Publications Company   Minneapolis

The author wishes to thank Mike Bisk, general manager and coach, and the entire coaching staff at the Coneja Gym Center; Gary Toner and Lee Standish at the Matador Gym Institute; Colleen and her mother, Beryl Loughlin; and the parents of all the children who participated in this project.

LIBRARY OF CONGRESS CATALOGING IN PUBLICATION DATA

Washington, Rosemary G.
Gymnastics is for me.

(The Sports for Me Books)
SUMMARY: A young gymnast demonstrates basic tumbling skills which she combines into routines to perform in competition.

1. Gymnastics—Juvenile literature. [1. Gymnastics] I. Oddie, Alan. II. Title. III. Series.

GV461.W37 1979   796.4'1   79-4496
ISBN 0-8225-1078-2

Manufactured in the United States of America

International Standard Book Number: 0-8225-1078-2
Library of Congress Catalog Card Number: 79-4496

4   5   6   7   8   9   10   90   89   88   87   86   85   84   83

Hi! I'm Colleen. If you are anything like me, I'm sure you watch sports on television. My favorite sport is gymnastics. It is even part of the Olympic games. I love to watch gymnasts perform. They are so graceful. Gymnasts compete in four areas — the balance beam, uneven parallel bars, vaulting horse, and floor exercise. I can't decide which competition is the most exciting.

3

Someday I'd like to be one of those gymnasts on television. But it will take years of practice before I am good enough. Right now I am only a beginner in the sport. I take lessons at the Gynmastic Center in town.

The center has all of the proper equipment for gymnastics. This includes safety mats in case you fall. It is really important to use the right equipment every time you practice. It is also important to have a good coach. My coach is Mr. Larkin.

We begin each practice with a warm-up
period. We exercise to loosen up our muscles
and to get in shape. We do push-ups and
sit-ups, touch our toes, and run.

It is a good idea to wear a warm-up suit
while exercising. A suit will keep you warm
and your muscles loose.

Gymnasts need strong arms and legs. We develop these parts of our bodies in a weight training program. We work to lift weights up and down, over and over.

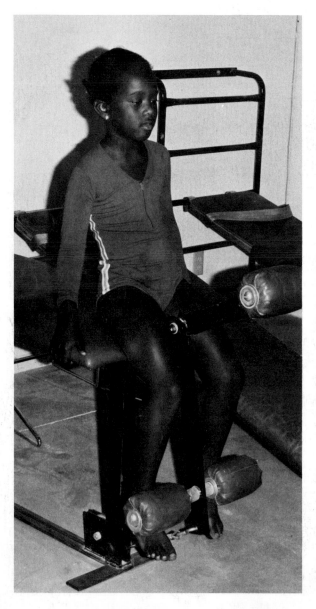
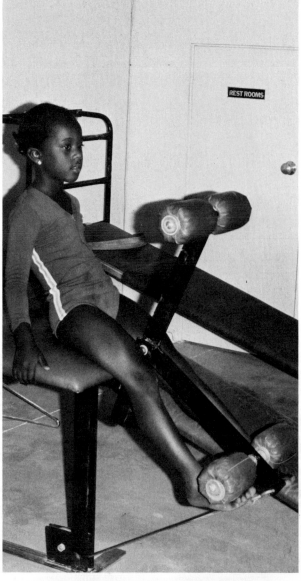

We do other exercises to stretch our muscles and make us more flexible. One stretching exercise is called the **pancake**, because you hug the floor. Another good one is the **trunk-bending exercise**. Gymnasts have to be flexible to do even basic gymnastic skills. Coach Larkin said we must always warm up with stretching exercises before working on any equipment.

THE PANCAKE

TRUNK-BENDING EXERCISE

You should work hard to show proper form even when you are just practicing. Otherwise it is easy to develop bad habits. This is important when exercising, too, because some exercises are just like positions you can do on the equipment or floor exercises. You can do stretching exercises like the front and side splits, for example, on the balance beam.

When you are first learning an exercise or a gymnastic move, you should have a **spotter** to help you. A spotter is someone who stays nearby and can offer a helping hand. A spotter can break your fall or catch you if you lose your balance.

Gymnastics is not an easy sport. It combines a variety of balance and tumbling skills. You have to practice hard to learn the basic skills. They will be used again and again on the balance beam, vaulting horse, uneven parallel bars, and in floor exercise. So it is important to be able to do the basic skills perfectly.

SCALE

HEADSTAND

HANDSTAND

Y-SCALE

Good balance is a must for any gymnast. Some basic balancing skills are scales, Y-scales, headstands, and handstands. When you do them, extend your legs, back, and arms as far as you can. A spotter should help you with your headstands and handstands. Keep your back straight and your toes pointed up.

13

FORWARD ROLL

Two of the most basic tumbling skills are **forward** and **backward rolls**. When you go into the tucked position, keep your big toes, ankles, and knees together. Your chin should be tucked into your chest so that the back of your head does not touch the floor. When coming out of a roll, reach forward with your arms to help yourself stand up.

BACKWARD ROLL

Always remember to have proper form at the finish as well as at the start of your roll.

Variations of the forward and backward roll are done on every piece of gymnastic equipment. Some variations are more difficult than others. In the floor exercise, for example, a gymnast may **somersault**, or do a roll in the air.

15

CARTWHEEL

Cartwheels and round-offs are some other basic tumbling skills. You must be able to do them from the left as well as from the right.

When doing a cartwheel, keep your legs straight and your toes pointed as I am doing here. You must travel in a perfectly straight line.

ROUND-OFF

A round-off is similar to a cartwheel. You start them both in the same way. But when your legs swing into the air for a round-off, you must snap them together. Make a quarter turn from the handstand position. Then, keeping your legs together, bring them back down to the mat.

Springs and walkovers are other important gymnastic skills. Jenny is demonstrating a **front walkover** in the pictures above. She starts the walkover like a handstand. But she splits her legs, bringing her feet down to the mat one at a time.

FRONT HANDSPRING

18

The **front handspring** that Mary Ann is doing below starts out like a handstand. It must be done quickly to give your body enough momentum, or push, to land on your feet. First kick your legs up over your head. Keep your legs together. Then spring off your hands before your feet swing back to the mat. You should land upright.

We practiced all the basic skills over and over until we could do them perfectly. Then we were ready to try some of the moves on the gymnastic equipment.

Gymnastic routines in the floor exercise and on the balance beam, the vaulting horse, and the uneven parallel bars combine a variety of skills. In a routine, the moves are performed one after another without stopping. You should practice all the moves on the floor before you try them on the equipment.

This is the balance beam. You must learn to keep your balance on this wooden beam, which is only about four inches wide. In a routine, you must keep moving and use every part of the beam.

Before practicing dance and tumbling moves on the beam, be sure there are mats on the floor below. And always have a spotter nearby.

You have to do a **mount** to get onto the beam at the start of your routine. There are lots of different mounts you can use. Pam is doing a jump to a "straddle" support. In any straddle movement, your legs are spread apart.

Once you are on the beam, you must be able to walk along it and to change directions. When walking, it is best to keep your eyes straight ahead. With lots of practice, you will know where the beam is without looking at it.

One way to change directions on the beam is to do the **pivot turn**. You just stand on your toes and twist your body around without moving the balls of your feet off their spots on the beam. You will then be facing in the opposite direction.

Your routine on the beam should include fast moves and slow ones. Some moves should be difficult. You can include balance skills, such as handstands or the scale opposite. You can also include leaps and tumbling skills.

Jenny shows good form on her forward roll, below. It is important to grasp the beam firmly with both hands. If you don't wobble, you will roll in a straight line and land correctly. You should use a spotter for rolls and other tumbling moves until you gain confidence.

This is the vaulting horse, which gymnasts must jump over. They gain momentum for the jump by taking a long, fast running approach. A takeoff board at the end of the run gives vaulters added lift.

In competition, a girl contestant does two vaults. Her best score is recorded. Vaults are scored on correct performance as well as on difficulty.

We began training for this event with two simple vaults—the **straddle vault** and the **squat vault**. In vaulting, the hands are the only parts of the body to touch the horse. But when we were first learning to vault, we landed briefly on the horse with our feet.

STRADDLE VAULT

SQUAT VAULT

Later we learned more difficult vaults like this **handspring vault**. Your run up to the horse should be smooth and fast. As you hit the takeoff board with both feet together, bend a little at your knees, hips, and ankles. With a powerful spring, straighten your legs and swing your arms up.

The actual vault begins when your hands touch the horse. Keep your body in good form with your toes pointed and legs

HANDSPRING VAULT

straight. Push off the horse with your fingertips, not your arms. Your elbows should remain straight throughout the vault.

The landing is an important part of every vault. You should land standing as straight as possible. You may have to bend a little at the knees and ankles. But do not step forward once your feet hit the mat. Keep your head and arms up.

These are the uneven parallel bars. Gymnasts perform graceful swinging moves around the bars. Their routines should include work on both the upper and lower bars. Here Michelle is **casting**, or swinging her body away from the lower bar.

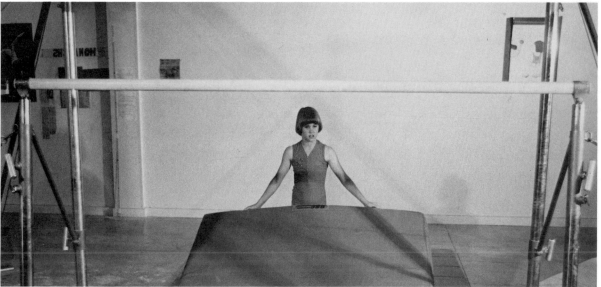

Before you begin practicing on the bars, you should adjust them to your height. Coach Larkin helps me with this. You should also be sure that there are mats on the floor below the bars. To prevent your hands from blistering, it helps to rub them with gymnastics chalk.

There are many different circling movements you can make around the bar. This one is called the **mill circle**. Your hands should grasp the bar from behind. Keeping your elbows and back straight, lift your weight onto your hands. Extend one leg in front of you and the other behind so that you are straddling the bar. With your legs in this position, move forward and downward, swinging the upper part of your body below the bar. With practice, you should be able to circle the bar in this position and return to your starting position.

You can also do support and balance positions on the bars. Here is Shelley doing a front support and a handstand. Remember not to hold any one position too long. Your routine should flow from move to move smoothly without stops.

The floor exercise is my favorite gymnastic event. Here tumbling and dance movements are set to music. Routines are done on a large square mat. The entire area should be used. You should not stay in one spot too long.

A good floor exercise has a variety of tumbling moves. The moves should flow smoothly together. A good way to connect different moves is to do some dance steps in between. Dance steps look graceful. Studying ballet is helpful because it can improve your form and body control.

Leaps are other moves you can include in
your floor exercise. Try to get good height
on your leaps. Remember to always point
your toes and extend your arms.

The rest of your routine should show your tumbling skills. Include some difficult moves. You should also change the pace of your routine. Mix fast moves with slow ones.

Good gymnasts practice their floor exercise, parallel bars, vaulting, and balance beam skills until they are good in all four events. In competition, gymnasts are judged in all events. A bad score in even one event could hurt your chances at winning.

My gymnastic center competes in the county meet each year. Eight of the center's best gymnasts make up the team. I was happy to be on the team this year.

At the meet, each person's performance was judged on a 10-point scale. A perfect score was 10. Gymnasts could win ribbons for doing the best in one event.

The teams also competed for ribbons. To get the team score, all the members' scores were added together.

The county meet had both boys' and girls' competitions. The boys' teams competed first. As we watched them perform, the girls stretched and warmed up to get ready for their events.

Male gymnasts compete in the floor exercise and vault just like girls do. But the boys also have other events that girls do not compete in—the side horse, rings, parallel bars, and horizontal bar.

The side horse looks like a vaulting horse with handles on it. Gymnasts make swinging leg circles around it. Routines on the side horse require balance and smooth motions.

Boys also perform on rings that hang from the ceiling. The gymnasts perform a variety of swinging, hanging, and balancing moves, like the **shoulder stand** and **pike hang** pictured above. In a pike position, you bend at the waist, keeping your legs straight forward. During each of the moves, the rings should remain still.

Boys' parallel bars are set at an even height. Gymnasts performing on the bars do swinging moves and holds. They must also do a strength move, like the shoulder press to a handstand.

The horizontal bar is one of the most exciting boys' events. Moves are performed on a slender metal bar high off the ground. Gymnasts make giant swings and circles around the bar.

When the boys' events ended, I knew it would not be long before I had to perform. I was nervous. But I tried to concentrate on my routines.

Performing was more fun than I thought
it would be. I did not forget even one step
in my routines. And I did not fall. When I
felt myself doing well, I began to relax.

I received high scores in all of my events. Out of 42 girls, I came in ninth in total points. Several of my teammates scored well, too. And our team placed second in the meet. I was really happy. All of the hard work had paid off. I'm glad I am a gymnast. I might even make it to the Olympics someday!

Words about GYMNASTICS

AERIAL: A move done completely in the air

CARTWHEEL: A tumbling move in which the body flips over sideways

CAST: To thrust or swing your body away from its point of support

COMPULSORY ROUTINE: A competition routine in which certain moves must be performed

DISMOUNT: A move used to get off a piece of gymnastic equipment at the end of a routine

FRONT SUPPORT: The act of supporting your body weight on your arms, which are held straight and rigid

HANDSPRING: A tumbling move in which the body is flipped quickly from a normal standing position to a handstand, and then back to an upright position

HANDSTAND: A position in which you balance on your hands with your feet straight up in the air

HEADSTAND: A position in which you balance on your head and hands with your feet straight up in the air

L-SUPPORT: A position in which your body is supported by straight arms at a right angle to your legs, which are parallel to the floor

MOUNT: A move to get onto a piece of gymnastic equipment at the beginning of a routine

OPTIONAL ROUTINE: A routine that is created by the gymnast and coach

PIKE: A position in which you bend at the waist and keep your legs straight forward

ROUTINE: A combination of tumbling, balance, and dance moves performed in sequence without stopping

SALTO: An aerial somersault

SCALE: A standing position in which you balance on one leg

SOMERSAULT: A complete rollover move

SPOTTER: A person who assists a gymnast and guards against injury

STRADDLE: A position in which your legs are spread wide apart

47

ABOUT THE AUTHOR

ROSEMARY G. WASHINGTON, an avid sports fan, is a freelance writer and graphic designer living in Seattle. She graduated from the University of Minnesota and has been a staff editor and book designer for a juvenile book publisher.

ABOUT THE PHOTOGRAPHER

ALAN ODDIE was born and raised in Scotland. He now resides in Santa Monica, California. In addition to his work as a photographer, Mr. Oddie is an author and a producer of educational filmstrips.